Robotic Gorilla

By Paul Beck

Silver Dolphin Books
An imprint of the Baker & Taylor Publishing Group
10350 Barnes Canyon Road, San Diego, CA 92121
www.silverdolphinbooks.com

Robotic Gorilla is produced by becker&mayer!, Bellevue, Washington.
www.beckermayer.com

ISBN-13: 978-1-60710-776-7
ISBN-10: 1-60710-776-7

Manufactured, printed, and assembled in Shenzhen, China.

1 2 3 4 5   16 15 14 13 12

12443

Editors: Don Roff and Ben Grossblatt
Designers: Lisa M. Douglass and Eric Liu
Illustrator: Joshua Beach
Production coordinator: Jennifer Marx
Managing editor: Michael del Rosario
Product designers: Chris Tanner and Ryan Hobson
Product developers: Chris Tanner and Peter Schumacher
Technical illustrator: Ryan Hobson
Fact-checker: Frank M. Young

Image credits
Every effort has been made to correctly attribute all the material reproduced in this book.
We will be happy to correct any errors in future editions.

Pages 4–5: AgAnt © Tony Grift, Department of Agricultural and Biological Engineering, University of Illinois at Urbana Champaign. Pages 6–7: Gorilla skeleton © skullsunlimited.com. Pages 8–9: Western lowland gorilla mother with baby © Tom Brakefield/Photodisc Blue/Getty Images. Pages 12–13: Cyberhand © Associated Press/Fabio Muggi; gorilla using tool © Thomas Bruer/MPI-EVA/WCS. Pages 14–15: rHex and Scout II © Martin Buehler. Pages 16–17: Juvenile gorilla swinging on a vine © Michael K. Nichols/National Geographic/Getty Images; mother and baby gorillas © Frans Lemmens/Iconica/Getty Images. Page 19: Koko © Ron Cohn/The Gorilla Foundation/Koko.org; Coco the robotic gorilla © MIT Computer Science and Artificial Intelligence Laboratory. Page 21: Sony Aibo Dogs at RoboCup © Messe Bremen. Page 23: King Kong Escapes © 1967 Toho Company Ltd. Page 32: Gorilla © John Giustina/VEER/Getty Images. Cards and poster: gorilla and human skeletons © Encyclopaedia Britannica/Contributor/Getty Images; big gorilla © 007_Bond/iStockphoto; young mountain gorilla in tree © Guenter Guni/iStockphoto; western lowland gorilla with branch © Ronald van der Beek/Shutterstock; young western lowland gorilla © Ronald van der Beek/Shutterstock; baby gorilla and mother © Eric Gevaert/Shutterstock; family of gorillas © FAUP/Shutterstock; large silverback gorilla © Mike Price/Shutterstock; gorilla eating © FAUP/Shutterstock; gorilla posing © Elliot Hurwitt/Shutterstock; gorilla on lookout © Smileus/Shutterstock; yellow robots welding cars © Rainer Plendl; police robot © chalabala/Shutterstock; male robot thinking © Sarah Holmlund/Shutterstock.

Introduction

Gorillas are our cousins. Like us, they are primates. That puts them among our closest living relatives in the animal kingdom. They're big, hairy, and smart. They travel in peaceful groups during the day, eating as they go. They sleep at night in nests made of grass, branches, and leaves. Unfortunately, these fascinating creatures are endangered. Due to poachers and deforestation of their habitat, gorillas are vanishing along with the trees of their African forest home.

Robots are our creations. Some look like us, but most don't. They're machines we make for doing work or for entertainment. Some experimental prototype robots can even help us learn how to build better, more advanced robots.

In this book you'll explore the natural world of gorillas and the technological world of robots at the same time. You'll see how gorillas have inspired robot creators to invent new robots. And you'll go ape as you put together your own robotic gorilla!

TABLE OF CONTENTS

Simulating Humans and Animals

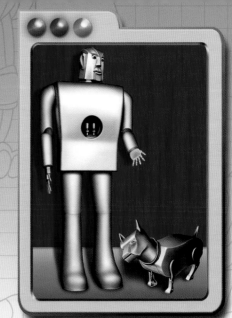

Elektro and Sparko

Robots are machines. All machines do work, but robots are special in the way they work and the type of work they do.

What Makes a Machine a Robot?

To start with, robots work by themselves or by remote control. A regular car isn't a robot, but a computerized car that drives itself is a type of robot. Industrial assembly-line robots work all day long, automatically. They pick things up, move them, put them together, take them apart, or carry them.

Other robots, however, need human help. Bomb-disposal robots work by remote control. NASA's Mars Exploration Rovers follow instructions from Earth, but they figure out on their own how to navigate from one place to another over different surfaces, and navigate around obstacles. They perform a combination of automatic and remote-controlled functions.

Most robots have sensors that tell them about their environment. Some sensors are very simple, such as one that detects when the robot has bumped into a wall. Other sensors are more complicated, such as radar or 3-D video-camera systems.

Animal Robots

People have been making machines that look and act like animals for a very long time.

Over 2,400 years ago, Archytas of Tarentum, a Greek mathematician, made a mechanical dove out of wood. The dove could supposedly fly with the help of a jet of air or steam.

In 1939, the New York World's Fair featured a robotic dog named Sparko, the companion of Elektro, a giant mechanical man.

In the early 1950s, scientist W. Grey Walter conducted experiments in robotic autonomy, or independence, with a pair of turtlelike robots named Elmer and Elsie.

Today, robotics scientists use all kinds of animals as models for experimental robots. There are roach-bots, snake-bots, dog-bots, fish-bots, dinosaur-bots, lobster-bots, bat-bots, and many others. And, of course, there are gorilla-bots, but you'll find out more about those later.

AGRICULTURAL ROBOTICS

AGRICULTURAL ROBOTICS, ALSO KNOWN AS "AGBOTS," IS A TECHNOLOGY WHERE SCIENTISTS ARE TRYING TO DEVELOP A MORE EFFICIENT WAY TO HARVEST FOOD CROPS. THE "AGANT" IS ONE SUCH ROBOT. IT WOULD WORK TOGETHER WITH A SIMILAR GROUP OF ROBOTS, PERHAPS TO PULL UNWANTED WEEDS OR PICK BEANS. ONE DAY, THE FOOD YOU EAT MIGHT BE "HANDPICKED" BY A ROBOT!

Robots are programmed by humans to follow instructions. These instructions may be simple commands like "go forward" or "turn around." The robots can also be programmed by computers that allow the robot to solve problems or explore a room by itself.

Robots repeat themselves, which can be a tremendous advantage. Factory robots, unlike human workers, do the same tasks over and over, all day long, without getting tired, bored, or needing a break.

5

What Is a Gorilla?

It's not hard to recognize a gorilla—they are a familiar sight at zoos and on television. Gorillas are large apes; in fact, they're the largest and most powerful of all primates. Primates are an order (a large group of related animals) that includes humans, apes, monkeys, tarsiers, lemurs, and others.

Great Apes

Gorillas belong to a family of primates known as hominids. Other hominids include humans and chimpanzees. After chimps, gorillas are our next closest relatives.

On average, male gorillas are about 5½ feet tall and weigh 400 pounds, but they can be as heavy as 600 pounds. Females are around 5 feet tall and weigh between 160 and 200 pounds. The big difference in size between males and females affects the way gorillas live. In a group of gorillas, big males have the most power.

Gorillas have black skin, and their hair is black or brownish-black. Their bodies are covered with hair except on their faces, hands, and feet. As a male gorilla gets to be about 12 years old, a patch of hair on his back turns silvery-gray, and he is then known as a silverback.

Female gorillas are fully grown and able to have babies when they are around 10 years old. Males usually don't become fathers until they are about 15. In the wild, gorillas can live to be 35 to 40 years old.

Adult gorilla skeleton

gorilla hands, gorilla feet

Like you, gorillas have five-fingered hands with opposable thumbs for gripping. Unlike you, gorillas also have opposable big toes, so they can grab onto things with their feet.

YOU MIGHT HAVE TO STUDY GORILLAS FOR A WHILE BEFORE YOU CAN TELL THE DIFFERENCE BETWEEN THE VARIOUS TYPES. MOUNTAIN GORILLAS HAVE LONGER HAIR THAN EASTERN LOWLAND GORILLAS. WESTERN GORILLAS HAVE BROWNISH HAIR ON THEIR HEADS AND ARE SOMEWHAT SMALLER THAN BOTH TYPES OF EASTERN GORILLA.

Gorilla Types

Gorillas live in African forests near the equator. There are two species: the eastern gorilla (*Gorilla berengei*), and the western gorilla (*Gorilla gorilla*). Mountain gorillas are a subspecies of eastern gorillas living in mountain forests in Rwanda, Uganda, and the Democratic Republic of the Congo. Eastern gorillas live in lowland forests nearby. Western gorillas live in lowland forests on the west coast of Africa. The main visible differences between the species are variations in coloring and size.

Congo · Uganda · Rwanda

GENERAL DISTRIBUTION

Go, Gorilla, Go!

Gorillas are constantly on the move, searching for food. They also raise their young while they travel. Both require special adaptation skills.

Gorilla Food

Gorillas receive their nutrition mainly from plants. Lowland gorillas also eat insects. Different gorilla types live in different environments, so they have different types of plants in their diets.

Mountain gorillas eat the stems, leaves, and shoots of plants. With their agile hands, they can peel apart stems to get to the soft pith inside. Bamboo is one of their favorite foods, especially the tender shoots. Mountain gorillas don't eat much fruit.

Eastern lowland gorillas eat the same types of plants as mountain gorillas, along with a lot of fruit. They also eat insects. Ants are their favorite insect snack.

Fruit is an even bigger part of the western gorilla's diet. They also eat plants that grow in swampy areas and streams. Western gorillas eat ants and termites, too.

Gentle Giants

In the old days, people who had never seen real gorillas thought they were fierce, bloodthirsty creatures that would attack unsuspecting explorers or carry off damsels in distress. Thanks to the scientists who study these apes in the wild, we now know that they are peaceful animals. Males will try to frighten intruders by slapping their hands against their chests, screaming, and charging, but these actions rarely turn into real fights.

Hungry?

Gorillas need a lot of food. A big male can eat as much as 40 pounds of plants in one day.

Studying Gorillas

Much of what we know about the lives of wild gorillas comes from the scientific work of Dian Fossey. Dr. Fossey spent more than 18 years observing gorillas at her research station in the mountain forest of Rwanda. The gorilla troops in the area got to know her and would let her get very close. Dr. Fossey's studies helped people understand the gorillas' day-to-day behavior, interactions, and habits. She also helped save thousands of African gorillas by establishing stricter antipoaching laws.

A gorilla family in its typical environment

GORILLA BABIES

MOTHER GORILLAS HAVE ONE BABY AT A TIME. LIKE A HUMAN BABY, THE BABY GORILLA TAKES ABOUT NINE MONTHS TO DEVELOP IN ITS MOTHER'S WOMB. GORILLAS ARE MUCH SMALLER THAN HUMAN BABIES WHEN THEY'RE BORN, BUT THEY GROW UP FASTER. BABIES STAY WITH THEIR MOTHERS FOR FOUR OR FIVE YEARS. THEY ARE FULLY GROWN WHEN THEY ARE ABOUT 10 OR 12 YEARS OLD.

On the Move

Gorillas live in family groups called troops. The usual size of a troop is about eight or nine, but some can include as many as 20 or more gorillas. The troop leader is a silverback male. There are sometimes other, younger males, but the silverback is the boss. The rest of the group consists of females and their children.

Troops are nomadic, moving around from place to place in search of food. The group never stays in the same place for more than a day.

Gorillas are diurnal, meaning they are awake during the day, although they take a nap in the middle of the day. At night, each gorilla sleeps in its own bowl-shaped nest of plants and leaves. Mothers sleep with their babies. Each gorilla makes a new nest every night.

Gorilla Parts and Robot Parts

Gorillas and robots can both be called "mechanical." A gorilla's machine is made of muscles, bones, and connective tissue, while a robot is made of pneumatic tubes, wires, and sensors. Though one is living and the other is not, they both function in similar ways.

Brain/Robot Controller

The gorilla's brain is the command and communication center of its body. It controls the gorilla's actions, takes in information from the outside world, learns, and solves problems.

The robot's "brain" is a special computer called a robot controller. It controls the robot's movements and takes in information from the sensors. In advanced robots, the controller can solve problems such as navigating around obstacles. Some robots' controllers even let them learn. But compared to a gorilla's brain, a robot controller is very simple.

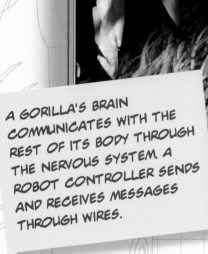

A GORILLA'S BRAIN COMMUNICATES WITH THE REST OF ITS BODY THROUGH THE NERVOUS SYSTEM. A ROBOT CONTROLLER SENDS AND RECEIVES MESSAGES THROUGH WIRES.

Senses/Sensors

A gorilla gets information about the world from its senses of sight, hearing, smell, taste, and touch. The information detectors are the gorilla's eyes, ears, nose, tongue, and skin.

Robots get their information through sensors. Video cameras are a robot's eyes. Microphones give it a sense of hearing. Smell and taste come from chemical detectors, and touch sensors can "feel" things. A gorilla has sense organs for all five senses, but some robots may only have one or two types of sensors. However, futuristic robots may incorporate all five senses.

HOW A ROBOTIC GORILLA MIGHT IMITATE THE MOVEMENTS AND CHARACTERISTICS OF ITS BIOLOGICAL COUNTERPART.

Muscles/Actuators

A gorilla's large muscles move its arms, legs, and all the other parts of its body. A gorilla wields enough muscular power to rip a car tire in two.

A robot's "muscles" are called actuators. Depending on the robot, the actuators may be electric motors, hydraulic (fluid-powered) or pneumatic (air-powered) cylinders, or a combination.

getting around

Both gorillas and robots need to be able to move around in their environments. Gorillas use their arms and legs for walking and climbing. Some robots walk on legs, too. Others have wheels or treads. Still others have wings for flight or fins and propellers for moving underwater.

Hands/End Effectors

Like humans, gorillas are good with their hands. Fingers allow the gorilla to grasp and hold objects. They can also do delicate work, like taking apart a plant to get to the parts the gorilla wants to eat.

Robot hands and tools are called end effectors. These are specially made for the job the robot has to do. The effector may be used like a hand for gripping. Or it may be a tool, such as the welders and paint sprayers found on assembly-line robots.

Handy Hands

Gorillas use their hands to hunt, manipulate tools, and climb. Robots can have hands to perform specific functions, too.

Feeling Fingers

When you use your own hands, you don't even think about it. Grabbing and holding onto things can be difficult for a robot. To make Robonaut good at gripping something as delicate as a potato chip, scientists are working on hand and finger sensors to give the robot a sensitive grip. One day, a robot may be able to emulate the sensitivity of human touch.

Handy Gorillas

In 2004, scientists studying gorillas in the Republic of the Congo made an amazing discovery. They watched as a female gorilla broke a branch off of a tree and used it to test the depth of the water as she waded into a pond. As she waded farther in, she used the branch as a walking stick. It was the first time anyone had seen a wild gorilla using a tool.

About a month later, the scientists watched another gorilla break off the dead trunk of a shrub and use it to hold herself up as she dug for water-dwelling plants. Later, she put the trunk down and used it as a bridge to walk across a patch of swampy ground.

Handy Robots

Just like humans, gorillas can use tools because they have hands. Hands make it easy to use different tools. If you're holding a wrench and you want to use a screwdriver, you simply put down the first tool and pick up the second.

On the other hand, most robot tools are attached to the end of the robot's arm. It's not easy to switch tools, and the tools need special attachments to fit into the arm. For this reason, robots can't use regular human tools.

Scientists at NASA are working to solve this problem with Robonaut, a robot astronaut designed to work with humans and human tools. Robonaut has hands like ours, complete with a thumb and fingers. With hands for gripping, Robonaut can use the same tools as human astronauts, as well as the handholds the astronauts use for moving around on the outside of a spacecraft. No special robot tools or fittings are needed.

A COMMON TREE BRANCH IS A USEFUL TOOL FOR A GORILLA. NOT ONLY CAN IT BE USED TO TEST WATER DEPTH, BUT IT CAN ALSO BE USED TO GATHER INSECTS TO EAT. THIS DEMONSTRATES HIGHLY DEVELOPED PROBLEM-SOLVING SKILLS FOR THE PRIMATE.

mind-controlled hand

A team of scientists in Italy have developed a robot hand that is controlled by brain power alone. In a month-long experiment, a man who lost his left hand and forearm in a car accident used his mind to move each of the hand's fingers separately and even grab and hold onto objects. The robotic hand was controlled by electrodes connected to nerves in the man's arm. The hand itself wasn't attached to the arm, but one day soon there will be robotic replacement limbs that work just like the real thing.

Legs and Wheels

HOW MANY LEGS?

JUST LIKE ANIMALS, DIFFERENT ROBOTS WALK ON DIFFERENT NUMBERS OF LEGS, DEPENDING ON WHAT THEY WERE DESIGNED TO DO.

If you're designing a robot to move around in the natural world, a good place to start would be to study real animals. Copying from nature to create machines or materials is called biomimetics (BYE-oh-muh-MEH-tiks), which means "life-copying." Walking robots are one type of biomimetic machine.

Why Walk When You Can Drive?

A machine with wheels is a lot easier to make than one with legs, so why would you want a walking robot in the first place? For the same reason you walk up the stairs instead of riding your bike. Wheels are good for flat, smooth surfaces, but robots often have to go where it would be hard or impossible to roll. Some robots have treads like a bulldozer, but even treads can't move over big obstacles. In some places, legs are the only way to go.

bipeds

Two-legged walkers are called bipeds. These robots walk like humans or birds. Bipedal walking is hard, because when the robot picks up one foot to take a step, it only has one foot left on the ground. Most two-legged robots are humanoid (humanlike), perhaps because humans are the ones who design them. Dr Robot was a humanoid robot designed to walk with a gait similar to that of humans and also has five fingers rather than the typical "robot pincer" grip.

Dr Robot

Hexapods and Octopods

Six- and eight-legged robots have an easier time walking than do robots with fewer legs. That's because they can pick up half their legs and still have enough feet on the ground to stand without balancing. Hexapod (six-legged) robots walk like insects, and octopod (eight-legged) robots walk like spiders or scorpions.

QUADRUPEDS

MOST QUADRUPEDS (FOUR-LEGGED ANIMALS) MOVE TWO LEGS AT A TIME WHILE WALKING. THAT MEANS THEY HAVE TO BALANCE ON THE OTHER TWO FOR A SHORT TIME WHILE TAKING A STEP. RUNNING OR GALLOPING ANIMALS MAY HAVE ALL FOUR LEGS OFF THE GROUND AT ONCE. SCOUT II IS A FOUR-LEGGED ROBOT THAT CAN WALK, TROT, GALLOP, AND EVEN GO UP AND DOWN STAIRS. IT CAN ALSO BOUND FORWARD USING ALL FOUR LEGS SIMULTANEOUSLY, AN ANTELOPE-LIKE WAY OF JUMPING KNOWN AS "PRONKING."

six-Leg switcheroo

This little robot called RHex has six springlike legs. Instead of bending at the hip and knee, the legs flip over the top like wheels with only one spoke. Normally, RHex walks on six legs, but in one experiment scientists gave the robot a new way of running. They got RHex to rear up and run along on its two hind legs. Running on two legs allows the robot to go faster while using less energy.

RHex

Walking and Climbing

Gorillas walk and climb using their hands and feet. Scientists have developed a robotic gorilla to walk and climb in the same fashion.

Walk Like a Gorilla

Gorillas walk on all fours. They support their weight in front on their knuckles, with their fingers curled into their palms. Only gorillas and chimps walk this way, which is called "knuckle walking." Gorillas hardly ever walk on two legs, but they will stand on two legs in order to use their hands.

Gorillas' arms are their longest and strongest limbs. If a gorilla held out its arms sideways, the distance between its hands would be longer than the length of its body. The long arms let gorillas walk partially upright, even though they're walking on all fours.

Adult silverback gorilla

Gorilla-bot

To move like a gorilla, a robot has to walk like a quadruped but be able to stand like a biped. Scientists at the University of Salford in England built a robotic gorilla to do just that. The robot is about the size and shape of a female lowland gorilla. The machine doesn't have any "skin," so it looks more like a framework gorilla than a real one. The gorilla-bot walks on all fours. Like a real gorilla, it can balance on two legs to use its arms to work with objects.

One of the ways the robotic gorilla imitates real life is in the actuators that move its arms and legs. The robot's "muscles" are pneumatic, or air-powered. Most pneumatic actuators are hard tubes with pistons. When air goes into the cylinders, the pistons push outward.

up in the trees

Gorillas spend most of their time on the ground, but they are good at climbing trees to get fruit or just to play. Smaller females and young gorillas climb easily into the branches. Big males can weigh as much as a quarter of a ton, so they don't climb as often. When they do, bigger gorillas stay on sturdy branches close to the trunk.

Taking refuge in the trees

However, the gorilla-bot's air-powered muscles are flexible. When air goes into them, these actuators get shorter and fatter, imitating the contraction of real muscles.

Swing-bot

Gorillas get around by walking, but some of their ape cousins have another way of traveling. Orangutans and gibbons move through the trees by using their arms to swing from branch to branch. Monkeys travel in this way, too. The scientific name for this mode of travel is brachiating (BRAY-kee-ate-ing). Scientists in Japan have invented an experimental robot that moves in this way.

Extra

Sensory

Scientists have developed special sensors in robots to emulate those of gorillas.

Coco

Scientists at the Massachusetts Institute of Technology (MIT) developed an experimental gorilla-like robot named Coco. Built like an ape, Coco had a broad chest, long arms, and short legs. Since the robot had no hands, it couldn't walk on its knuckles, but it did walk on all fours like a gorilla. The robot had a pair of video cameras for eyes.

Coco was quite a bit smaller than a real gorilla. The robot weighed 20 pounds and stood about a foot and a half tall. Its motors, sensors, and the electronics that run them were inside the body, but it took a whole bank of computers to act as Coco's brain. They were connected to the robot's body by a computer network cable.

This little gorilla-bot was designed to explore and learn about its environment by itself, without instructions from humans. The robot got information about its surroundings from its sensors, which gave it the senses of sight, hearing, and touch.

Koko

Coco is a robotic gorilla, but Koko is a real gorilla. Koko is a nickname for Hanabi-Ko, which is Japanese for "fireworks child." Koko the gorilla was born on July 4, 1971.

Koko is a famous gorilla because she has learned to communicate using American Sign Language, or ASL. ASL is a language used by many deaf people in the United States. Instead of spoken words, ASL uses signs made by the hands. Gorillas can't speak words with their voices, but their hands can form the word signs of ASL.

Dr. Francine Patterson, the scientist who studies Koko, has been teaching and talking with the gorilla since Koko was a baby.

extra sense

Coco also had a sense of balance. A gyroscope and gravity sensor told the robot about the position of its head. This let Coco keep its eyes level to the ground.

Coco was an experiment to create a robot that could interact with humans. One of the aims of the project was to give Coco the ability to show emotions like curiosity and fear. These emotions affected whether the robot would approach or avoid things in its environment.

Autonomous Robots

Robots that work by themselves, without step-by-step instructions from humans, are called autonomous (ah-TAHN-uh-muss) robots. The word comes from the Greek for "self-ruling." Coco is an autonomous robot.

Coco

ROBOBABBLE

IT TOOK A LOT OF INTENSE TRAINING TO TEACH KOKO THE LANGUAGE SIGNS SHE KNOWS. BUT HUMAN BABIES LEARN TO TALK WITHOUT SPECIAL TRAINING. BABIES START BY LISTENING, LEARNING THE SOUNDS OF THE LANGUAGE THAT'S BEING SPOKEN AROUND THEM. NOW SCIENTISTS HAVE DEVELOPED A ROBOT THAT LEARNS LANGUAGE SOUNDS THE SAME WAY. AT FIRST THE ICUB ROBOT SIMPLY BABBLES, BUT AS PEOPLE TALK TO IT THE WAY THEY WOULD TALK TO A BABY OR TODDLER, THE ROBOT LEARNS TO REPEAT LANGUAGE SOUNDS AND WORDS.

Real and Artificial Intelligence

Gorillas and robots are both intelligent. Gorillas use natural—or real—intelligence. A robot's intelligence, however, must be programmed into it. This is called artificial intelligence, or AI.

Smart Apes

Koko's sign language gives scientists a special opportunity to find out about gorilla intelligence. They can't do this with other animal species. It takes a pretty good brain just to learn over a thousand word signs. Gorillas can figure out how to use simple tools, and they can learn from other gorillas just by watching them.

Smart Machines

Most robots aren't smart at all. That is, they can follow programs, even very complicated ones, but they can't solve problems on their own, and they can't learn new things by themselves. The average robot isn't even as smart as the average cockroach.

Scientists in the branch of computer science that deals with artificial intelligence are working to make smart computers and robots. The goal of AI is to build machines that can solve problems, learn, and even think.

machine intelligence test

The British mathematician Alan Turing came up with a test to see whether a machine is intelligent. To test the machine, he suggested placing a machine and a human in separate rooms. The tester asks both of them questions. If the tester can't determine from the answers which is the machine and which is the human, the machine must be intelligent. To date, no machine has passed the test.

Smart Ape-Machine

Lucy is a robotic ape. She isn't modeled after a gorilla, but rather after the gorilla's primate cousin, the orangutan. She has a computer "brain" that can learn on its own, without programmed instructions.

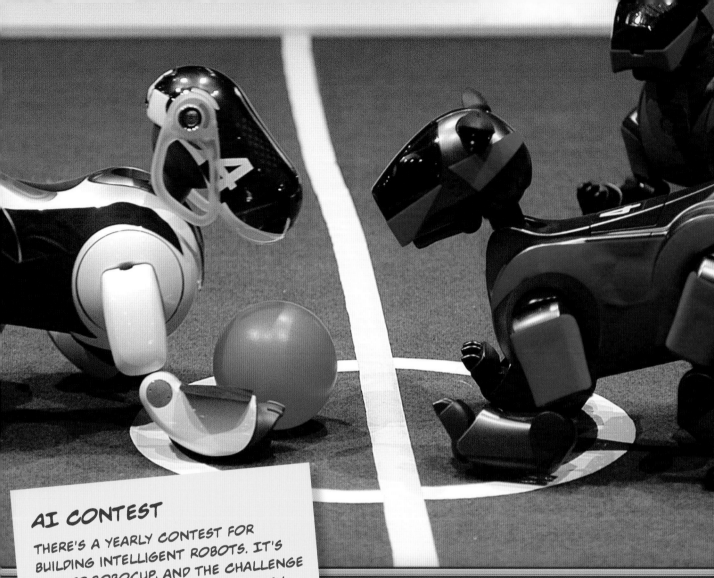

And what was Lucy's big achievement? When shown an apple and a banana, she learned to point to the banana. This might not seem like a big deal, but it's more than other robots can do. Lucy was programmed to prefer bananas, but the robot learned by itself how to recognize the two fruits, tell the difference between them, and point to the long, yellow one.

JUST FOR THE ASKING

Some scientists believe Koko's word signs give them a way to find out about gorillas' intelligence in a new way. They can ask her questions, and she can answer them. Dr. Patterson, Koko's trainer, has given the gorilla human intelligence tests and has found that Koko is not very far below the average human intelligence.

Reel
Gorillas

There's one type of robot that isn't made for doing work. Instead, its purpose is to be a real-looking, moving, mechanical version of an actual animal or person. These are referred to as animatronic (AN-i-muh-TRON-ik) devices. You can often see animatronic creatures at amusement parks or museums. Some of the most realistic are used in movies and television.

Gorillas in the Movies

Gorillas are a popular feature on the big screen. In the old days, it was because people thought they were dangerous monsters, and people enjoy monster movies. Nowadays, it may be because gorillas are like us—but at the same time just different enough to make interesting or funny stories. Gorillas are strange and familiar at the same time.

King Kong

The most famous movie gorilla is Kong, a giant ape who was taller than a three-story house, more than five times the size of a real gorilla. Kong made his first appearance in the 1933 movie *King Kong*. There were no animatronics when the movie was made. The giant, menacing gorilla was animated in 3-D, using a movable model that was just 18 inches tall.

Kong Again . . .

King Kong was remade in 1976, 43 years after the original. The remake was supposed to featu 40-foot-tall robotic gorilla. The robot was built, but it looked and worked so badly that it only appeared in a couple of brief shots.

In this remake, an actor in a gorilla costume played the part of Kong. But the costume was fake-looking gorilla suit. The face was an animatronic mask. Cables operated by puppeteers w muscles of the gorilla's face. They gave the mask realistic expressions and face movements.

The movie also featured a pair of giant robotic gorilla hands for close-up scenes. Each han big enough to hold an adult human and took six people to operate.

. . . and Again!

Yet another remake of *King Kong* was released in 2005, but this time the giant gorilla was ani by means of computer graphics.

ROBOTIC KONG

King Kong was a popular attraction at Universal Studios in California. On the tour, a 40-foot-tall "life-sized" King Kong—operated by hydraulics and electronics—terrorized visitors. The robotic Kong was unfortunately destroyed in a fire in 2008.

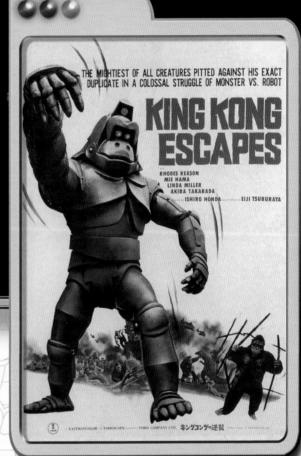

THE MIGHTIEST OF ALL CREATURES PITTED AGAINST HIS EXACT DUPLICATE IN A COLOSSAL STRUGGLE OF MONSTER VS. ROBOT

KING KONG ESCAPES

RHODES REASON
MIE HAMA
LINDA MILLER
AKIRA TAKARADA

ISHIRO HONDA   EIJI TSUBURAYA

King Kong Escapes, a 1967 Japanese science fiction film

The Future of Robotic Gorillas?

Can you foresee a day where there might be a real, working robotic gorilla? Instead of going to Universal Studios and seeing an animatronic King Kong stuck in one place and repeating the same motions, imagine seeing a robotic gorilla that could walk among the tourists, entertaining them. Or perhaps someday a robotic gorilla could be manufactured to perform serious work, like rescuing people from high places that a helicopter or ladder couldn't reach. As long as gorillas possess the power to inspire scientists to build better robots, the possibility of seeing a fully automated robotic gorilla someday is a real one.

Assembly Instructions

before you begin

Take all the parts out of the package and lay them on a flat surface.
Read through all of the assembly instructions.

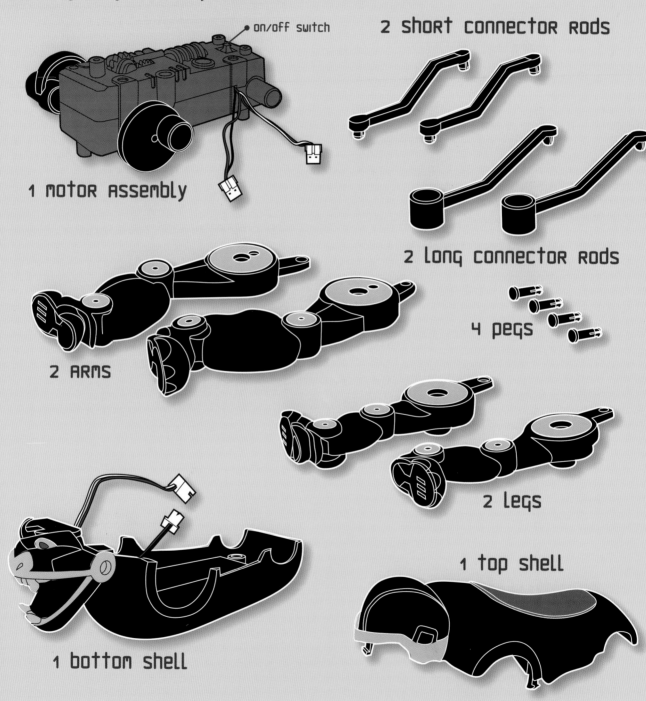

on/off switch

1 motor assembly

2 short connector rods

2 long connector rods

4 pegs

2 arms

2 legs

1 bottom shell

1 top shell

Make sure that the jaw lever is *under* the motor wheel.

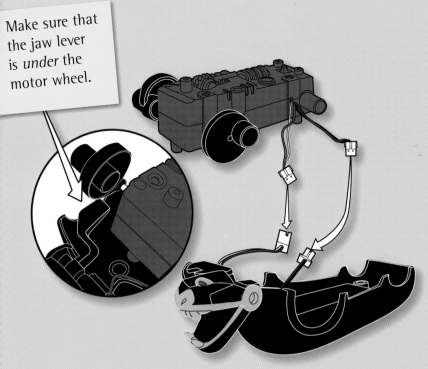

1. install the motor assembly

▸ First, connect the blue/white wire plug of the motor to the blue/white wire plug of the shell. Then, connect the red/black wire plug of the motor to the red/black wire plug of the shell. And finally, insert the motor assembly into the bottom shell.

▸ Carefully fit the wires alongside the motor assembly as you place the assembly in the shell.

2. attach the top shell

▸ Place the top shell onto the bottom shell. The tabs on the top shell fit into the holes on the bottom shell. Start by inserting the back tab of the top shell into the back hole of the bottom shell, then insert the front tab.

Make sure you don't pinch any wires between the top and bottom shells!

3. Assemble and Attach the Left Leg

▸ Connect the left leg to the long connector rod by pushing a peg through the holes. (Look for the Ⓛ on the inside of the leg to identify which is the left leg.) Next, fit the hub of the connector rod and left leg assembly onto the rear left hip axle. Push the peg through the leg and into the axle to connect it.

hub

axle

The connector peg must fit into the leg slot at the hip.

axle

shaft

4. Attach the Left Arm

▸ Insert the left arm shaft into the front shoulder axle. (Look for the Ⓛ on the inside of the arm to identify which is the left arm.) Insert a peg and push it in until it snaps into place.

5. Connect the Long Rod

▶ Snap the end of the long connector rod into the eyebolt of the left arm.

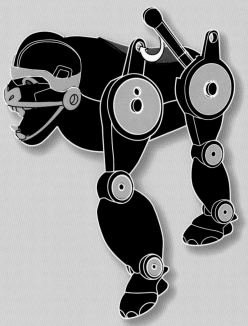

6. Connect the Short Rod

▶ Insert the pegs of the short connector rod: first into the hole in the front shoulder and then into the eyebolt on the leg.

7. Assemble and Attach the Right Leg

▶ Connect the peg of the right leg to the hole in the connector rod. Next, fit the hub of the connector rod and right leg assembly onto the rear right hip axle. Push the peg through the leg and into the axle to connect it.

To allow proper movement of the gorilla, ensure that the long connector rod is seated within the notch of the leg.

7. Assemble and Attach the Right Leg

▶ Connect the right leg to the long connector rod by pushing a peg through the holes. (Look for the ® on the inside of the leg to identify which is the right leg.) Next, fit the hub of the connector rod and right leg assembly onto the rear right hip axle. Push the peg through the leg and into the axle to connect it.

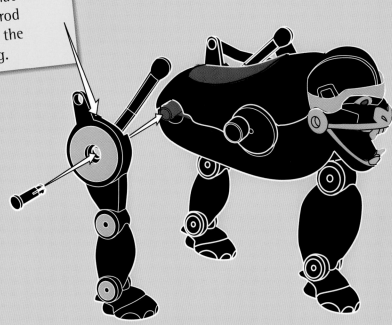

Assembly Instructions

8. Attach the Right Arm

▸ Insert the right arm shaft into the front shoulder axle. (Look for the ® on the inside of the arm to identify which is the right arm.) Insert a peg and push it in until it snaps into place.

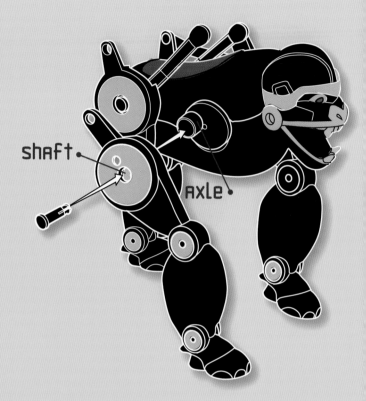

shaft

axle

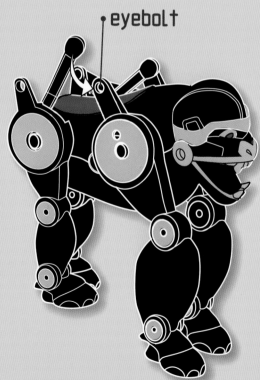

eyebolt

9. Connect the Long Rod

▸ Snap the end of the long connector rod into the eyebolt of the right arm.

10. connect the short rod

▸ Insert the pegs of the short connector rod; first into the hole in the front shoulder and then into the eyebolt on the leg.

11. insert the batteries

▸ Unscrew the battery compartment door (only three or four turns should be necessary). Remove the door. Insert two AAA batteries into the battery compartment according to the markings inside the compartment. Make sure you insert them the correct way. Screw the battery compartment door back on.

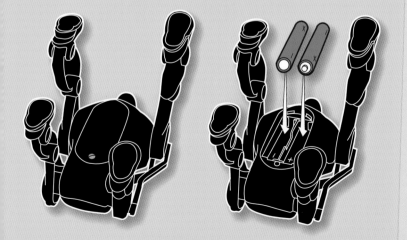

battery cautions

✓ To ensure proper safety and operation, the battery replacement must always be done by an adult.
✓ Never let a child use this product unless the battery door is secure.
✓ Keep all batteries away from small children, and immediately dispose of any batteries safely.
✓ Batteries are small objects and could be ingested.
✓ Nonrechargeable batteries are not to be recharged.
✓ Rechargeable batteries are to be removed from toy before being charged.
✓ Rechargeable batteries are only to be charged under adult supervision.
✓ Different types of batteries or new and used batteries are not to be mixed.
✓ Only batteries of the same or equivalent types as recommended are to be used.
✓ Do not mix alkaline, standard (carbon-zinc), or rechargeable (nickel-cadmium) batteries.
✓ Batteries are to be inserted with the correct polarity.
✓ Exhausted batteries are to be removed from the toy.
✓ The supply terminals are not to be short-circuited.

Making Your Gorilla Walk

▶ Press the clear hatch (on/off button) on the back, and the gorilla should walk forward on its arms and legs with lighted eyes and a snapping jaw action. The gorilla will move best on a smooth, flat surface. Turn the gorilla off by pressing the clear hatch (on/off button) again.

things you can do with your gorilla

You've learned about the gorilla and the robots it has inspired. Now you've constructed a robotic gorilla of your own. You're ready to experiment and find out what your gorilla can do.

to push and to pull

▶ How much pushing power does your gorilla have? Can it knock over small objects such as paperback books? Can it budge objects along the floor or across a tabletop? Your gorilla might turn aside when it bumps up against an obstacle—can you construct something it can push straight forward? Maybe it pulls better than it pushes. Connect objects to its rear end with a piece of tape. Switch it on and see how well it performs. How heavy do the objects have to be before the gorilla can no longer walk?

into the nitty-gritty

▶ Try out your robotic gorilla in some dirt or sand. How does the gorilla's footprints look different from your footprints? How do the design of the robotic gorilla's feet and hands help it balance and walk? Be careful, excess dirt or sand in the motor could affect the gorilla's performance.

up the hill

▶ Set your gorilla on a tilted surface—like a board propped under a book—switch it on, and watch it climb. How steep can the surface be before the gorilla can't climb anymore? How steep does it have to be before the gorilla slips back down to the bottom? Do you think your gorilla can walk downhill as well as it walks uphill? Try it and find out.

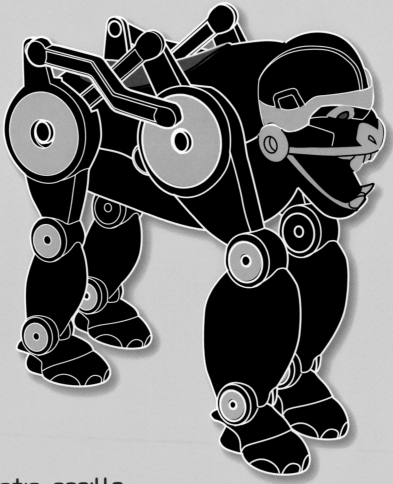

assembled robotic gorilla

Your assembled robotic gorilla should look like this. Have fun!

troubleshooting

If you've followed these assembly instructions and your gorilla doesn't work correctly when you switch it on, follow these tips.

If your gorilla doesn't walk smoothly:

▸ Make sure the batteries are inserted correctly.

▸ Make sure the batteries are fresh.

If your gorilla doesn't walk at all or the lights don't come on:

▸ Make sure the batteries are inserted correctly.

▸ Make sure the batteries are fresh.

If your gorilla turns on but doesn't walk:

▸ Make sure the connector rods are fitted properly to the arms and legs.

Amazing Gorilla Facts

Adult silverback gorilla

▶ Gorillas are the largest living members of the primate family, a group of related animals that includes humans.

▶ After chimpanzees, gorillas are humans' next-closest living relatives.

▶ An adult male gorilla can eat as much as 70 pounds of food in a day.

▶ A gorilla never sleeps in the same nest twice.

▶ No one has ever held a gorilla strength contest, but some scientists estimate that a strong silverback male may be as much as eight times more powerful than a strong man.

▶ Humans can be identified by their fingerprints. Gorillas can be identified by their nose prints! No two gorillas have the same nose prints.

▶ Gorilla babies develop physical skills about twice as fast as human babies.

▶ An adult male gorilla can spread his arms as wide as 8 feet from fingertip to fingertip. A female's arm span is 6½ feet.

A mother and baby gorilla

▶ Gorillas can make more than 20 different sounds with their voices.

▶ The oldest gorilla in captivity is Colo, at the Columbus Zoo in Ohio. She was born in 1956.

THE WORD "GORILLA" IS SAID TO COME FROM A WORD IN AN ANCIENT AFRICAN LANGUAGE THAT MEANT "HAIRY PERSON." IT WAS FIRST MENTIONED MORE THAN 2,500 YEARS AGO IN A STORY ABOUT THE VOYAGE OF AN EXPLORER NAMED HANNO, FROM THE ANCIENT CITY OF CARTHAGE.